Karen's Little Witch

**Look for these
and other books about Karen
in the
Baby-sitters Little Sister series:**

Little Sister

Karen's Little Witch

Ann M. Martin

Illustrations by Susan Tang

A
LITTLE APPLE
PAPERBACK

SCHOLASTIC INC.
New York Toronto London Auckland Sydney

ISBN 0-590-44833-1

Copyright © 1991 by Ann M. Martin. All rights reserved. Published by Scholastic Inc. APPLE PAPERBACKS is a registered trademark of Scholastic Inc. BABY-SITTERS LITTLE SISTER is a trademark of Scholastic Inc.

12 11 10 9 8 7 6   5 6/9

Printed in the U.S.A.   40

First Scholastic printing, October 1991

For my parents and my sister

Karen's Little Witch

Morbidda Destiny

Hum, de-hum, de-hum.

I was sitting at my desk in my classroom. I was looking at my teacher, Ms. Colman. I had noticed that one of her earlobes was larger than the other.

Hum, de-hum, de-hum.

I was not *supposed* to be staring at my teacher's earlobes and humming. I was supposed to be filling in a math worksheet. That's what everyone else was doing. But I had finished. I hoped my friends would finish soon, too.

Ms. Colman stood up. (I could not see her earlobes as well.) She asked us to hand in our worksheets. When we had done that, she said, "Guess what, class. I have an announcement to make."

Yippeeeee! Ms. Colman's announcements are usually surprising. I just love Surprising Announcements.

Oh, by the way, I am Karen Brewer. I am seven years old. Ms. Colman is my second-grade teacher. I am the youngest kid in my class. That is because I skipped a grade.

Ms. Colman is the first teacher I have met who makes Surprising Announcements.

"Class," said Ms. Colman, "I know it is not October yet, but we should start thinking about Halloween. In a few weeks — "

"Oh, Ms. Colman! Oh, Ms. Colman!" I cried.

"Indoor voice, Karen," Ms. Colman reminded me patiently.

"Sorry. I want to know if we can have a Halloween party."

2

"As a matter of fact," Ms. Colman said, "our school is going to have one big party. We are going to have a costume parade, too. Your families will be invited to watch."

"Cool!" cried Ricky Torres. (Ricky sits next to me. Once, we got married on the playground.) "I want to be a gumball!"

"You can dress as a gumball when you go trick-or-treating," said Ms. Colman. "But every class is being given a costume theme for the parade. Our theme will be Favorite Story Characters."

Goody, I thought. That was perfect. Every year I dress up as a witch. I have never dressed as anything else. My witch costume is fantastic. (I am not bragging.) If we were supposed to dress like our favorite story characters, then I could be the Wicked Witch of the West from *The Wizard of Oz*. Or I could be the witch from *The Witch Next Door*.

I have quite a few books about witches. I love to read witch stories. Guess what. A witch lives next door to *me*. Honest. Daddy says she is just a funny old woman. He says her name is Mrs. Porter. I know better. She is a *witch* and her witch name is Morbidda Destiny.

Morbidda Destiny wears long black dresses. She keeps a broom on her front porch. She has a black cat named Midnight. She planted an *herb garden* in her backyard.

I am pretty sure that I have seen Morbidda Destiny ride her broomstick out of a bedroom window and fly into the night.

I am afraid of Morbidda Destiny.

So are my friends Hannie Papadakis and Nancy Dawes. Hannie and Nancy are my *best* friends. We call ourselves the Three Musketeers. We are all in Ms. Colman's room. (But Nancy and Hannie get to sit in the back row. I have to sit in front with the kids who wear glasses. The glasses-wearers in my class are Ricky, Natalie Springer, Ms. Colman, me.)

Anyway, even if I am afraid of witches, I do not mind living next door to Morbidda

Destiny. That is because I don't have to live next door to her very often. Only two week-ends each month, and on some holidays and vacations. The rest of the time I live with my mother and stepfather.

Two Families for Karen

M_y parents are divorced. They do not live together anymore. (This happens sometimes.) Mommy and Daddy used to be married. When they were married, they loved each other. So they had me. Then they had Andrew. (Andrew is my little brother. He is four going on five.) After awhile, my parents decided they did not love each other anymore. They loved Andrew and me but not each other. So they got a divorce.

Mommy and Daddy and Andrew and I

used to live in a big house. It was the house Daddy grew up in. After the divorce, Mommy moved into a little house. (Both of the houses are right here in Stoneybrook, Connecticut.) Andrew and I moved with her. Then Mommy got married again. She married Seth. He is my stepfather. Seth lives with us at the little house. So do his cat, Rocky, and his dog, Midgie. And so does my rat, Emily Junior.

Daddy got married again, too. He married Elizabeth. She is my stepmother. Elizabeth already had four children! They are my stepbrothers and stepsister. Charlie and Sam are old. They go to high school. David Michael is seven like me. But we go to different schools. David Michael goes to Stoneybrook Elementary. I go to a private school called Stoneybrook Academy. My stepsister is Kristy. She is thirteen. I *love* having a big sister. Kristy is one of my most favorite people in the whole wide world. She can baby-sit. Sometimes she baby-sits for David Michael and Andrew and me.

Also for Emily Michelle. Emily is my adopted sister. She is two and a half. Daddy and Elizabeth adopted her. She comes from a country called Vietnam. Someone *else* lives with my big-house family. That is Nannie. She is Kristy's grandmother, so she is my stepgrandmother. Nannie takes care of Emily while Daddy and Elizabeth are at work. Some pets live at the big house, too. They are Boo-Boo (Daddy's old tiger cat), Shannon (David Michael's puppy), and Goldfishie and Crystal Light the Second (Andrew's and my goldfish).

Andrew and I live mostly at the little house with Mommy and Seth. But every other weekend we live at the big house. Andrew and I do not mind going back and forth. We like having two families. (I call us Karen Two-Two and Andrew Two-Two. I made up those names after Ms. Colman read a book to our class. The book was called *Jacob Two-Two Meets the Hooded Fang*.) Andrew and I are two-twos because we have two of so many things. We have two houses and two mommies and two daddies and two cats and two dogs. We have toys at the little house and toys at the big house. Same with books and clothes. And I have two bicycles, one at each house. And two stuffed cats. Moosie lives at the big house, Goosie lives at the little house. Guess what. Hannie is my big-house best friend. She lives across the street and one house down from Daddy. Nancy is my little-house best friend. She lives next door to Mommy. See why I like being a two-two?

Well, I like being a two-two *most* of the time. But not always. I do not have two of *every*thing, of course. I have only one pair of roller skates. And I used to have just one Tickly, my special blanket. I kept leaving Tickly behind at one house or the other. Finally, I had to rip Tickly in half so I could keep a piece at each house. (I hope that did not hurt Tickly.)

Also, when I live at the little house, I miss Crystal Light the Second and my big-house family. And when I live at the big house,

I miss Emily Junior and my little-house family.

Another thing I have only one of is Morbidda Destiny. No witch lives next door to the little house. That is fine with me. A part-time witch is enough.

3

Ghouls and Goblins

" 'Bye, Mommy!" I cried.

" 'Bye, Mommy!" cried Andrew.

"See you later, alligators!" said Mommy.

"After awhile, crocodile!" Andrew and I replied.

Mommy had driven my brother and me to Daddy's. It was a big-house weekend. We had arrived just in time for Friday night supper.

"Come on, Andrew," I said.

I closed the car doors. Mommy drove away. Andrew and I walked to the big house. We were each wearing a knapsack. And I had remembered my skates.

Suddenly, the front door began to open. I had not even touched it!

Inside, the hallway was dark.

"Helloooooo," wailed a voice. "Do not beeeeeee afraaaaaaaid. Pleeeeeease come in."

"Is today Halloween?" Andrew asked me.

"No," I said. "And the door did not open by itself, either. David Michael is standing behind it. I can see him." (I couldn't really see him, but I knew he was there.) I marched inside. "Hi, David Michael," I said loudly.

"Very funny." David Michael stepped into the hall. He turned on a light. "Hi, Professor," he greeted me. (He calls me "Professor" because of my glasses.) "Hi, Andrew."

"Hello! Hello!" The rest of my big-house family came to meet Andrew and me.

"I hope you two are hungry," said Nannie.

"Hey, Karen, your epidermis is showing," said Sam.

"Sam. I already know that joke. You taught it to me. Epidermis is skin."

"Just testing," said Sam.

Andrew and I put our knapsacks in our rooms. Then we went to the kitchen for dinner with Daddy, Elizabeth, Nannie, Kristy, Sam, Charlie, David Michael, and Emily. I got to sit next to Kristy.

"Well, Halloween is almost here," I announced while we were finishing dinner.

"It is?" said Andrew.

"Not for a month," said Charlie.

"Of course, I am going to be a witch again," I said.

"Of *course*," replied David Michael.

I looked across the table at Andrew. "Oh, witchy, witchy, witchy," I murmured.

"Karen," warned Daddy.

"I didn't do anything!"

"Yes, you did. You are singing witch songs," cried Andrew.

"You know, tonight's a full moon — " I began.

"Karen, you may be excused," said Daddy.

Darn. I had learned a good Halloween story to tell Andrew. Now I would have to wait. At least I had already eaten my dessert.

I went to my room. I sat on my bed and looked out the window.

There was the full moon.

There was Morbidda Destiny's house.

A light was on in an upstairs room. Was it the witch's bedroom? I turned off my own light so I could see better.

There are not many rules at the big house, but one of the rules is NO SPYING ON THE NEIGHBORS. Well, sometimes I cannot help myself.

I couldn't see anything at Morbidda Destiny's house. But I remembered something I had seen a long time ago when I was six.

14

I had seen a meeting of witches and war-locks there. (Warlocks are boy witches.) Or I *thought* I had seen a meeting. I had never been sure. That's the problem with witches. You just never know about them.

4

Druscilla

When I woke up on Saturday morning, I thought, "What a peaceful night."

Sometimes I dream about witches. But I had slept well the night before. I did not remember any dreams at all.

" 'Morning, Moosie. 'Morning, Tickly," I said. (I always sleep with them. I hope I don't squish them or anything.)

I ran downstairs. In the kitchen were Elizabeth, Nannie, Andrew, and Emily. We ate breakfast together. Everyone else was still asleep. Except for Daddy.

"Where's Daddy?" I asked Elizabeth.

Elizabeth pointed out the window, into the backyard. "In the garden," she said.

"Oh, goody! I think I will help him today."

Daddy loves to garden. He has planted gardens all over our yard. But his special flower garden is in the back. Sometimes Daddy lets me dig holes for new plants. Or pull up weeds. Or water with a watering can. I like watering the best. That is gigundo fun. (I know lots about gardening because once I visited my grandparents on their farm, which is in the state of Nebraska.)

After breakfast I got dressed in gardening clothes. I put on my overalls and a shirt and my straw hat. (I bought the overalls and the hat in Nebraska.)

"Hi, Daddy," I said. "I'm here to help you."

" 'Morning, Karen. Do you feel like watering?"

"Oh, yes!"

Daddy showed me which plants needed to be watered. I got right to work. I walked all around the garden with the can. I was at the back of the garden when I heard Daddy say, " 'Morning, Mrs. Porter!"

Mrs. Porter? Yipes! The witch!

If I ran through the yard and into the house, would Morbidda Destiny see me? I wondered. Probably, since she's a witch. I decided to try it anyway. But before I had put down the watering can, I heard Daddy say, "Karen? Honey? Come say hello to Mrs. Porter."

So I had to say hi to the witch. She was wearing a long, black dress, as usual. And her gray hair was all frazzly.

Morbidda Destiny does not always say much. But that morning she talked a lot. She said, "Have you heard the news? My family is moving to Stoneybrook. My daughter and her husband and their little girl. Druscilla is your age, Karen. She's seven. Actually, Druscilla is coming first," continued the witch. "Her parents want

20

her to start in her new school as soon as possible. She'll be here in just a few days."

"Her new school?" I repeated.

"Stoneybrook Day School."

I let out a sigh of relief. Druscilla would not be going to *my* school.

But then the witch said, "Druscilla will live with me for a few weeks."

"Really?" I squeaked.

This is what I was thinking. If Mrs. Porter is a witch, then her daughter must be a witch. And if her daughter is a witch, then *her* daughter must be a witch. So Druscilla was a witch. *Two* witches would be living next door to Daddy's house! A big witch and a little witch.

Daddy let me leave then. I tore across the street. I ran to Hannie's house. Then Hannie and I ran to Melody's house. Melody is our new friend. She just moved here. Melody is seven, like Hannie and me. But she goes to . . . Stoneybrook Day School. The witch's school.

"Maybe the little witch will even be in your *class*," I said to Melody. "Morbidda Destiny said Druscilla is seven."

"Oh, no," said Melody. "She *can't* be in *my* class!"

5

She's He-ere!

I was sort of glad to go back to the little house on Sunday. There are no witches near Mommy's house. No big witches, no little witches. Even so, I could not stop thinking about witches.

In school on Monday, Hannie and I told Nancy about Druscilla.

"Yipes," said Nancy. "I wonder when she will arrive."

She arrived sometime on Tuesday. I know because Melody called me on Wednesday night. She said, "Karen! The

23

little witch is here! She was in school today."

"In your class?" I cried.

"No. But she's next door," said Melody. "She is in the other second-grade room."

"What does she look like?" I asked.

Melody lowered her voice. "Like a witch," she whispered.

"Really?" I said. I said that because sometimes Melody's imagination runs away with her.

"Yes. Her eyes are very dark. Almost black. And her hair *is* black. It's long and wild, too. But her skin is pale," said Melody.

"Like Snow-White's?"

"Yes. Just like Snow-White's. And all her clothes are black."

"Ooh. All of them?"

"Well, I did not see her underwear. But her dress and her tights and her shoes were black. And in her hair was a black ribbon."

"Very witchy. Did she cast any spells?" I asked.

24

"No. At least, I did not *see* her cast any spells. But I only saw her twice. In between, she had plenty of time to cast spells."

"Hmm."

"Oh, but wait!" exclaimed Melody. "I almost forgot about Druscilla's lunch."

"Her lunch?"

"Yes. She ate a *mushroom* sandwich."

"Oh. Gross. Mushrooms. She *must* be a witch."

"That's what I thought," said Melody.

Mommy called to me then. She said it was bedtime. "I have to go," I told Melody. "But I'll see you soon. I'm going to Hannie's after school on Friday. And I will be at Daddy's on Saturday, even though it is not a big-house weekend."

"Goody," replied Melody. "Maybe you will see the little witch for yourself."

6

The Little Witch

On Friday afternoon, I got to ride home with Hannie. (I just love playing at my friends' houses.) Hannie's brother, Linny, rode home with us. And Hannie's little sister, Sari, was sitting in her car seat. Hannie and I squished into the back seat with Sari. Linny got to ride up front with Mrs. Papadakis.

"What are you going to do today?" Linny asked. He turned around to look at Hannie and me. (He crossed his eyes.)

"Don't answer him," Hannie whispered to me. "He wants to pester us."

"I do not!" exclaimed Linny. "Mom, Hannie says I am going to pester her."

"See what I mean?" said Hannie. "He is already pestering us."

When we got to Hannie's house, Linny was still acting like a great big pain.

"We have to escape from Linny," Hannie whispered.

"Can we have a snack first?" I asked. "I'm starving."

"Okay," agreed Hannie. "Then we will escape. Where should we go?"

"Over to Melody's," I answered. "She can tell us more about the little witch."

So Hannie and I ate some Scooter Pies. (My mommy will not buy Scooter Pies.) Then we went to Melody's house. Melody was sitting on her front steps. She was reading a book called *The Pain and the Great One*.

"Hi, Melody!" I called.

Melody put down her book. She and Hannie and I sat under a tree.

"Have you seen Druscilla again?" I asked Melody.

"Yes." Melody nodded her head. She looked quite excited. Then she glanced across the street — at Morbidda Destiny's house.

"What is it?" asked Hannie. She looked across the street, too.

"I am pretty sure now," said Melody, "that Druscilla is a witch."

"You are?" I cried. "What did you see?"

Melody lowered her voice. "I saw Druscilla wave her hand. Then — BANG — out of nowhere came this big bunch of flowers. She gave the flowers to her teacher."

"Are you sure?" I exclaimed. I did not wait for Melody to answer. "Then Druscilla *must* be a witch!"

"Let's go spy on her," said Melody.

"Oh. We better not. I am not allowed to spy on the neighbors," I told Melody.

28

"Who says?"

"Daddy."

"Well, you are at *my* house now, and I say we can spy."

Melody and Hannie and I ran across the street. Then we ran to this big bush in front of Morbidda Destiny's house. We scrunched down behind it.

"Does anyone see Druscilla?" I asked.

"Nope," said Hannie and Melody.

We hid for the longest time. We watched and watched. Finally . . .

"Someone's coming out the front door!" I hissed.

Melody and Hannie and I leaned over as far as we could.

"It's Druscilla! It's the little witch!" said Hannie.

"*Shhh!*" said Melody. "What's she doing?"

Druscilla sat on the steps of the front porch. She rested her chin in her hands. She looked a little lonely. A few moments later, Midnight wandered over to Druscilla.

29

She patted his back. She scratched him behind the ears.

"The little witch and the witch cat," murmured Hannie.

"*SHHHH!*" hissed Melody again. "Do you want her to hear us?" Just then, Melody lost her balance. She fell down. She was not hidden by the bush anymore.

Druscilla looked up. She saw us! Quick as a flash, we ran away.

7

The Herb Garden

Hannie and Melody and I were lucky. We escaped from Druscilla. She did not cast a spell on us or anything. We were safe.

But the next day, I went back to Daddy's house. It was not a big-house weekend. But Mommy and Seth had to go to a town called Stamford. They were going to be there the whole day. So Andrew and I stayed with Daddy.

When Mommy dropped us off at the big house, I ran inside quickly. I was not taking any chances. I did not want Druscilla to know I was back.

At the big house, I got a surprise.

Daddy said to me, first thing, "Karen, today I would like you to go next door and visit Druscilla. She is feeling lonely."

Well, for heaven's sake. What was I supposed to do about that? And why was Daddy making me play with a witch?

"Karen?" said Daddy. "Did you hear me?"

I nodded. "Do I have to go?" I answered.

Daddy gave me a Look.

"Okay, okay," I said. "Um, could I eat breakfast first, though?"

"Didn't you eat breakfast at Mommy's?"

"Oh. Yes. I did. But I'm still hungry."

Daddy fixed me a piece of toast. I cut the crusts off of the edges. Then I ate a hole in the middle. I stuck my tongue through the hole. After that, I made holes for my eyes. I looked at Daddy through my toast-mask.

"Are you ready to go outside now?" asked Daddy.

"Yes," I answered. And I did go outside. But I did not go next door to the witch house. (Daddy had not asked if I was going to visit Druscilla.) Instead I went into our backyard. I walked all around. I scuffed through the leaves that had fallen. I looked at Daddy's gardens. I wished we had a swing set. (But we did not.)

I knew I would have to go to Druscilla's house sometime that morning. But I was not ready to go just yet. I was still a teensy bit afraid.

I scuffed through some more leaves. Then I heard a voice. I looked into Morbidda Destiny's backyard. Druscilla was standing in the herb garden!

Yipes!

I ducked behind a tree. Then I peeked around it. Druscilla was carrying a basket. She picked some leaves off of the herb plants. She put the leaves in the basket. The basket was half full.

What were those herbs for? I wondered. But I already knew the answer. They were for spells, of course. What else do witches do with herbs?

Well, that was that. I would *not* go to Morbidda Destiny's house alone. No way.

So I snuck out of our yard. I checked over my shoulder. Good. I was not being followed by any witches. I raced to Hannie's house. Hannie was in her room with Melody. They were playing with their dolls.

"You guys! I need help!" I exclaimed. "It's Druscilla, the little witch!"

"Uh-oh," said Hannie. "What happened?"

"She's in Morbidda Destiny's herb garden! She is picking herbs."

"Ooh. For a spell?" asked Melody.

"Yes," I replied. "*And* Daddy says I have to go over there today. He says I have to talk to Druscilla because she is lonely. Will you come with me? I cannot go alone. Not to a witch house."

Hannie looked at Melody. Melody looked at Hannie.

Finally Melody said, "Okay. We will come."

"But first we need some witch protection," added Hannie.

8

Boo!

"Witch protection is easy," I said. I turned to Melody. "Hannie and I make witch protection all the time. First you need some good-luck charms. And you cannot use charms you have used before."

"Let's go to Sari's room," suggested Hannie. "She has lots of stuff."

In Sari's room, we found a wind-up duck. We found a little stuffed ladybug. And we found a pink plastic block.

"Everybody choose one," said Hannie.

"Won't Sari mind?" I asked.

"Nah. She will never know."

Hannie took the ladybug. I took the block. Melody took the duck. We went back to Hannie's room. We said a magic spell (a *good* magic spell) over the charms. This is the spell we made up: *Abracadabra cadabra cadilla. Please let us be safe when we're near Druscilla.*

We put our charms in our pockets. We went back to my yard.

"Now tiptoe!" I hissed.

I tiptoed to the big tree. Melody and Hannie tiptoed behind me. I peered at the herb garden. It was empty. "She's gone," I said. "Come on, you guys."

We tiptoed into the herb garden. We looked around Morbidda Destiny's backyard. No big witch. No little witch.

"I think we're safe," I whispered.

"BOO!"

"Aughhh!"

Something had jumped up on the other side of the herb garden. (I had screamed.)

"Save me!" yelled Melody.

"It's just *me*." Druscilla walked around the garden.

Melody and Hannie and I almost fainted. We were too scared to move.

Druscilla walked so close to me that her black dress nearly touched my arm. "How come you guys wouldn't play with me yesterday?" she asked.

"I — I —" said Hannie. "I mean, we . . ."

"I *saw* you hiding," Druscilla went on. She turned to Melody. "And I see *you* every day in school. But you do not talk to me."

"I'm shy," Melody mumbled.

"Me, too," I said.

Then I took a good look at Druscilla. Her eyes and hair *were* black. And her skin *was* very pale. And her hair was wild, and her clothes were all black. Just like Melody had said.

"Excuse me, but are you a witch?" I could not help asking that question.

Druscilla paused. Then she said, "Yes!"

"I thought so." I nodded my head. "You have special powers, right?"

"Special witchy powers," agreed Druscilla. "Um, I can turn people into frogs. And . . . and . . . Well, I am just a kid witch. I cannot do *that* many things."

"So you can't do as many spells as your mother and your grandmother?" asked Hannie.

"As my mother and my — ? Oh, right," said Druscilla. "Right. They are better witches than I am. Because they are older."

"Can you ride a broomstick yet?" Melody wanted to know.

"Not yet. But when I grow up, I will ride as well as my grandmother does."

I glanced at Druscilla's basket. "I guess you know all about herbs, don't you?"

"I know more than most people do," agreed Druscilla. "If you want, I will show you what is in the garden. Look. Here is, um, witchwart. That's what gives witches their warts. And here is spellcast. And this is moonbroom, and this is . . ."

9

Pippi Longstocking

"How many of you are planning to go trick-or-treating this year?" asked Ms. Colman.

I raised my hand. So did every other kid in my class. I wondered why our teacher was asking about trick-or-treating. Soon I found out.

Ms. Colman held up a small cardboard box. It looked like a bank. A slot had been cut in the back. It was the perfect size for coins. The bank was decorated with Halloweeny pictures: a witch flying her broomstick in front of a full moon, a ghost sitting in the bare branches of a tree, and masks and candy and jack-o'-lanterns.

"Maybe," began Ms. Colman, "some of you would like to help others when you go trick-or-treating. If you take one of these banks with you, you can collect money for the hospital. All you have to do is hold out the bank and say, 'Trick-or-treat for the hospital.' Some people will give you money. The next day, bring your banks to school. We will count the money you collected, and then we will donate it to the hospital."

"What about our candy?" whined Hank Reubens.

"You can trick-or-treat for candy, too," said Ms. Colman. "Candy for you and donations for the hospital. The hospital needs some new equipment."

Trick-or-treat, trick-or-treat. Give me something good to eat, I thought. I pictured myself in my witch costume. I would wear my black, pointy witch hat and my black, fluttery witch dress and my black, clumpy

witch shoes. I would look just like Morbidda Destiny.

Or maybe I would look like Druscilla.

But do I *want* to look like Morbidda or
Druscilla? I wondered. I remembered
seeing the big witch fly out of her bedroom
window on her broomstick. I shivered.
Then I remembered the little witch in the
herb garden. Witchwart, spellcast, moonbroom. I shivered again.

"Boys and girls," said Ms. Colman,
"please raise your hands if you would like
to collect money for the hospital on
Halloween."

I raised my hand. So did a lot of other
kids.

"Wonderful," said Ms. Colman. She
smiled.

I tried to smile, too. But I couldn't.

"Ms. Colman?" I said. It was lunchtime.
My friends were getting ready to go to the
cafeteria. "I have to tell you something. I
have changed my mind. I do not want to

be the Wicked Witch of the West for Halloween after all."

"Who do you want to be?" asked my teacher.

"I'm not sure. But not a witch."

"Well, you may change your mind," Ms. Colman said. "But I do need to know which story character you will dress as in the parade. Can you make a decision in two days? Halloween is getting closer."

"I can make a decision," I said.

At home that afternoon I thought and thought.

What character could I be?

I looked at the books on my shelves. Paddington Bear? Nah. Peter Rabbit? Nah. Winnie-the-Pooh? Nah. I did not want to dress like an animal. Fur is too hot. Then I saw my copy of *Pippi Longstocking*. I could be Pippi! That would be fun. Pippi has two red braids that stick straight out. And her whole name is Pippilotta Delicatessa Windowshade Mackrelmint Efraim's Daughter Longstocking. I wish I had a name like Pippi's. And a monkey named Mr. Nilsson, like Pippi does. Being Pippi would be fun, even if it was only for a day.

10

No Way!

"*Oh, Pippilotta Delicatessa Windowshade Mackrelmint Efraim's Daughter Longstocking. That's me! That's me! That's me, me, me!*" I sang.

It was a Saturday morning at the big house, and I was very busy. I was getting ready for a tea party. My guests were going to be Hannie, Melody, Moosie, and Boo-Boo. Well, Boo-Boo might not stay long. He might have to leave early. He is not good at sitting still. (He could *never* go to school.)

I set the table in my room. I used every piece of my flowery china tea set.

The table looked gigundoly gorgeous.

"Hello! We're here!" called Hannie and Melody. They ran up the stairs.

"Oh, goody. We can begin," I said. "Let me just find Boo-Boo."

I found Boo-Boo, and I lugged him to the party table. I sat him in a chair. I put a napkin around his back.

FWOO! Boo-Boo ran away. He did not like the napkin.

"Oh, well. We do not need Boo-Boo," I said. "Besides, he is a boy."

"So is Moosie," pointed out Melody.

"Oh, yeah. But he is stuffed, so it does not matter. Come on. Let's be Lovely Ladies. Pinkies up while you drink your tea," I said.

Melody and Hannie and I put on our best manners. While we drank our pretend tea, Melody said, "You should have been at my school yesterday. The little witch made a cloud rain right on the playground. And

the day before? She turned her teacher upside down. Mr. Rowland had to walk on his hands for three hours. Druscilla has a magic wand."

"Are you kidding?" said Hannie.

"Oh, my gosh," I whispered.

"Knock, knock," said a grown-up voice. Daddy was standing in my doorway. "I'm sorry to interrupt your party," he said. "But I need to ask a favor. I was talking to Mrs. Porter this morning, and she was telling me how lonely Dru is. So, Karen, I would like you to invite Dru to go trick-or-treating with you."

Spend Halloween with the little witch? "No way!" I cried.

"Karen," said Daddy, "Dru is your neighbor. I want you to be nice to her. Remember your manners. Being new in town is not easy."

I was listening to Daddy. But I was thinking, No way, no way, no way . . .

11

The Little Witch's Party

What a gigundoly huge problem.

I just could not ask the little witch to trick-or-treat with me. Being with a witch on Halloween is dangerous. Plus, I did not want to go over to Morbidda Destiny's house to ask Druscilla *anything*.

How could I tell Daddy those things, though? *He* does not believe in witches. *He* does not think Mrs. Porter is a witch. *He* would certainly not think Druscilla was a witch. "She's a little girl," he would say.

I thought about my problem for the rest of Saturday.

I dreamed about my problem on Saturday night.

On Sunday morning, Daddy said to me, "Karen? Did you invite Dru to go trick-or-treating with you yet?"

"Um, no," I answered.

Daddy gave me a Look. The Look meant, "Please talk to Druscilla today."

All right. I did not have a choice.

Then I began to worry about something. If I went trick-or-treating with the little witch, would my friends come with me?

What if they would *not?* Yipes!

I ran to Hannie's house as fast as I could.

"Hannie! Hannie!" I cried. I dashed into her room. "Daddy says I *have* to invite Druscilla to come with me on Halloween. If I do, will *you* still come with me? You won't make me go trick-or-treating with Druscilla by myself, will you?"

"We-ell . . ."

"Oh, Hannie, you have to come with me. You *have* to! So does Melody."

"Let's go talk to Melody," said Hannie.

So we ran to Melody's house.

"Please, please, please, please, please, please, *please* come with me!" I begged.

"Maybe it would be okay," said Melody slowly. "We could protect ourselves again. Then we would be safe."

"And will you come with me now? While I talk to Druscilla?" I asked.

Melody and Hannie did *not* want to come. But they came anyway.

"Just remember our spell," I whispered. *"Abracadabra cadabra cadilla. Please let us be safe when we're near Druscilla.* We do not need the charms, I guess. Since we are in a hurry."

My friends and I left Melody's house.

We crept across the street to Morbidda Destiny's.

"Who's going to ring the bell?" I asked.

"You are!" hissed Melody and Hannie.

So I did. (My hand was shaking.)

The little witch answered the door. She looked as witchy as ever.

"Want to come trick-or-treating with us?" I said in a rush.

"Now?"

"No! On Halloween."

"Oh." Druscilla looked disappointed. "I want to. But I can't."

"You can't?" I tried not to sound too happy. I looked at Hannie and Melody, though. I could not help myself. We smiled at each other.

"No," said Druscilla. "I am going to have a party on Halloween night. My grandmother and I will give it. And you are all invited."

"We are?" I squeaked. I could not believe my ears.

"Can you come?" Druscilla wanted to know.

"Um . . . we have to ask our parents." Hannie and Melody and I left quickly.

12

Mr. Pumpkinhead

I was pretty sure that Daddy would say I had to go to Druscilla's party. I was right.

"But what about trick-or-treating?" I asked. "I am going to collect money for the hospital. I told Ms. Colman I would."

"You can go trick-or-treating first," replied Daddy. "Then you can go to the party."

"Oh."

Well, guess what. Hannie's parents said she had to go to the party, too. So did

Melody's parents. At least we would be there together.

When Halloween was just one week away, Mommy said, "I think it is time to buy pumpkins. Who wants to go to the farm?" (It was a little-house weekend.)

"Me!" cried Andrew and I.

"Me!" cried Seth.

I laughed. Seth just loves Halloween. Maybe he loves it even more than I do. I am not sure. Anyway, I was very excited when Seth said, "Today, jack-o'-lanterns. Tomorrow, we decorate the yard."

"Yeah! Can Nancy come to the pumpkin patch with us?" I asked.

"Of course," said Mommy.

"Pumpkins here, pumpkins there. Pumpkins, pumpkins everywhere!" I sang.

"We have to pick just the right pumpkins," said Nancy.

"I did not know there were this many pumpkins in the whole world," said An-

drew. He was looking at the pumpkin patch. We were standing in the very middle of it. All around us were bright orange pumpkins, in every shape and size.

"I want a fat, round one," said Nancy.

"I want a skinny one," said Andrew.

"I want a big one!" I exclaimed.

We looked and looked. When we had found a round pumpkin, a skinny pumpkin, and a big pumpkin, we went home.

That night, Seth said, "Time to carve the pumpkins!"

Andrew and I put our pumpkins on the kitchen table.

"I am going to make Mr. Pumpkinhead," I announced.

"I am going to make a goofy pumpkin," said Andrew.

Seth carved the tops off of our pumpkins. Their stems became handles for the lids. Then Andrew and I scooped out the seeds and the squishy pumpkin insides. We used big spoons.

"Who wants a snack?" asked Seth. He

showed Andrew and me how to separate the seeds from the gush. He spread the seeds on baking pans and he roasted them in the oven. Yum!

While the seeds roasted, Andrew and I planned our pumpkin faces. We drew them on paper. Then we drew them on the pumpkins. Then Seth helped us cut out the eyes and noses and mouths. I gave Mr. Pumpkinhead a big smile. I gave him round, wide eyes. I even gave him ears.

"Lovely," I said, when Mr. Pumpkin-head was finished.

"Goofy," said Andrew, looking at his pumpkin.

Seth put a candle in each jack-o'-lantern. He set Mr. Pumpkinhead and his friend in the living room window. He lit the candles and turned out the lights.

"Ooh," I said. The pumpkin faces glowed eerily. "I feel very Halloweeny. I am ready for ghosts and spooks and witches."

"And candy!" added Andrew.

13

"I Told You I Was Sick!"

"Are you ready to decorate for Halloween?" Seth asked.

Andrew and I had *just* woken up. We had not even eaten breakfast. But Seth was very excited about Halloween.

"How much decorating are you going to do?" Mommy wanted to know.

"Well," Seth began to say.

"Please do not go overboard," Mommy went on.

"I promise," said Seth.

But he winked at Andrew and me. I knew

we would do plenty of decorating. Just like we always did.

The first decoration we made was . . . a witch. Not just a paper witch to hang on our door. We made a lifelike witch. We gave her a long, dark robe, and a witch hat, and a broomstick. We sat her in the branches of a tree in front of our house. I stood behind the tree and said, "This is the witch speaking. Heh, heh, heh." (I did not mean to scare Andrew, but I did.)

When Andrew stopped crying, we made a huge ghost. We hung the ghost in another tree. The sheet fluttered in the breeze. When the ghost was finished, we made a *graveyard*. Honest! Andrew and Seth and I cut tombstones out of white cardboard. We wrote things on them like "Rest in Peace" and "Frank N. Stein." Seth even made a tombstone that said, "I told you I was sick."

In the afternoon, Nancy came over. She read the tombstones. She laughed. Her favorite one was "I told you I was sick."

Nancy helped us decorate. By the end of

the afternoon, the witch, the ghost, the graveyard, a black cat, and a skeleton were in our yard.

"We need a monster," said Andrew.

But Seth was tired of decorating.

"I'll teach you a monster song instead," offered Nancy.

"Goody," said Andrew.

Nancy and Andrew and I went to my room. We sat on my bed.

"This is a very silly song," said Nancy. "I heard it on the radio. This is how it goes: *I was working in my lab late one night, when my eyes beheld an eerie sight, as my monster from his slab began to rise, and suddenly to my surprise, he did the Mash! He did the Monster Mash!*"

" 'The Monster Mash'!" exclaimed Andrew.

"Yeah. It was a graveyard smash," added Nancy.

"Let's sing it for Mommy and Seth!" I exclaimed.

Nancy taught Andrew and me the words

to the song. Andrew kept saying, *"I was working on my slab late one night,"* and, *"He did the Smash!"*

Oh, well.

We were about to perform the song when I got a great idea. "Wait here!" I said to Nancy and Andrew. I ran to the kitchen. When I came back, I was carrying three spoons. "These will be our microphones!" I said.

Nancy and my brother and I gave our performances from the staircase. Nancy stood on the bottom step, Andrew stood two steps above her, and I stood two steps above him. We held up our microphones.

"I was working on my slab late one night," sang Andrew.

Mommy and Seth clapped for our song.

"Thank you," said Andrew. "You have just heard 'Monster Smash'!"

14

Pippi and Charlotte

"Oh, yippee! Oh, yippee! Oh, yippee!" I cried. "Tricks and treats aren't far away. Halloween is here today!"

That was not quite true. Halloween was the next day. But my rhyme sounded pretty good. I liked it a lot. Maybe I should add to it.

No! I did not have time. I had to get dressed and go to school. Usually, I can get dressed in about two minutes. But on that morning, I needed half an hour. I had to have time to put on my Pippi Longstocking costume for . . . the Halloween parade.

First I put on my long stockings. They were very tall socks. Mommy said, "Why don't you just wear tights, Karen?" But I wanted to be like Pippi. I mean, I wanted to *look* like her. (I already act like her.) Then I put on a dress like the one Pippi was wearing on the cover of my book. I put on big Pippi shoes, too. After that came the fun part.

Freckles! Mommy let me color big freckles across my cheeks and nose. I used her eyebrow pencil for that.

I looked at myself in the bathroom mirror. "Gigundoly beautiful," I said. "And now for the extra-special Pippi braids."

It is not easy to make braids that stick straight out from your head. Here is what I did. I leaned over. I let my hair fall toward the floor. I brushed it out. Then, while I was still leaning over, Mommy made two long "upside-down" braids. When I straightened up, they did sort of stick out from my head, although not as well as Pippi's. But I did not care.

"Do I look like Pippi?" I asked my family at breakfast.

"Definitely," said Seth.

"You could be her twin," said Mommy.

"Did Pippi look like a frog?" asked Andrew. (He was mad because he did not get to wear his costume to preschool. So I ignored him.)

Ding-dong!

"There's the doorbell!" I cried.

"Trick-or-treaters already?" asked Andrew.

"No, silly. It's Charlotte," I told him.

"Who's Charlotte?"

"Charlotte is really Nancy," I whispered. "But she will be wearing her spider costume. From *Charlotte's Web*."

Nancy's costume was terrific. Anybody would have known she was a spider. Her mommy and daddy helped her make extra legs. The legs stuck out of her tummy and

dangled down from her wrists. She wore a black leotard and a black hat. She was carrying a paper spider web. Written in the web was: SOME PIG!

"You look great!" I said to Nancy in the car. (Seth was driving us to school.)

"Thanks. So do you, Pippi."

"Why, thank you, Charlotte."

Seth stopped the car. Nancy and I ran into our school. Our classroom looked so funny! Sitting at the desks were a teddy bear, a cat, a princess, a farmer, even an elephant. (The elephant was Babar.)

We had a hard time thinking about work. So Ms. Colman let us color very special Halloween pictures. We colored designs on oaktag. Then we covered the designs with a layer of black crayon. Then we scratched pictures into the blackness. The colors underneath showed through. I drew a picture of me in the Halloween parade.

The Halloween Parade

I liked my picture of the parade. (So did Ms. Colman. She tacked it to the bulletin board.) But I was more excited about the real parade.

When recess was over, Ms. Colman said, "It is time to get ready for the parade. Who needs help with their costumes?"

A lot of kids raised their hands. So Ms. Colman helped them put on makeup and things like that. Soon it was time to line up to walk to the auditorium. I stood between Charlotte and the Cat in the Hat. (The Cat in the Hat was Hannie.) Guess what. Ms. Colman dressed as Mother Goose!

My friends and I walked into the auditorium. On the walls were pictures of ghosts and pumpkins and skeletons. In the seats were mommies and daddies and brothers and sisters. I could not see Mommy and Seth and Andrew and Daddy and Elizabeth and Nannie and Emily Michelle. But I knew they were there. They had said they would come.

All the kids in my school had a chance to show off their costumes. We paraded across the stage, class by class. One class was dressed as animals. Another class was dressed as cartoon characters. (I liked those costumes. It would have been fun to dress as Charlie Brown or Lucy or Elmer Fudd.) Another class was dressed as food!

I was very excited about parading across the stage. I could not wait to show off my costume. I hoped everyone would say, "Look! There's Pippi!"

Pretty soon Ms. Colman led my class to

the stage. Our principal said, "And now Ms. Colman's second-grade class will show us their storybook character costumes."

Ms. Colman walked across the stage. We followed her. The audience clapped for us. So I waved to them. While I was smiling at the audience, I found Mommy and Seth and Andrew. Andrew was wearing his costume! He was dressed as a Christmas elf.

I was so embarrassed. Nobody else's brother was wearing a costume.

I stopped waving.

But I was too late. Andrew had seen me. He waved back.

"Who's that kid?" Ricky Torres whispered.

"Nobody," I replied.

"Wait. Isn't that your brother?"

"I don't know."

When the parade was over, refreshments were served. Everyone got to drink cider and eat doughnuts and candy corn.

Andrew ran to me right away. "Hi!" he called. "Listen to me. I jingle!"

"I know you do," I said. (I had seen his costume about a hundred times.)

"Hey, Karen! That *is* your brother!" exclaimed Ricky Torres. "How come *he's* wearing a costume?"

I looked at Mommy. "Why did you let Andrew come to my school like that?" I asked her. (I decided not to say he was embarrassing.)

"Oh, honey," said Mommy. "He just wanted to wear his costume today. After all, you got to wear yours."

I thought about that. "Okay," I said finally. Then I whispered to Andrew, "I really like your costume. But don't stand near me. And whatever you do, do not tell anyone you are my brother."

"Okay," replied Andrew.

After that, we had a lot of fun at the party.

16

The Night
Before Halloween

Andrew and I stayed in our costumes for the rest of the day. He called me Pippi. I called him Kringle. (He had said his name was Kringle Jingle.)

We rode to the big house in our costumes.

We rang the big-house doorbell in our costumes.

When Kristy answered the door, we said, "Trick or treat!"

Kristy laughed. "Come on in," she said.

"You are just in time to help us decorate the front hall for tomorrow."

"We want it to look really spooky," said David Michael.

"We want to frighten the trick-or-treaters," added Sam.

"Oh, we do not," said Charlie. "Sam is kidding. We just want to make a fun spookhouse. Do you guys want to help?"

"Yes!" cried Andrew and I.

"First let's make a ghost," said David Michael.

"Maybe we can make him look like he's floating down the stairs," said Sam.

Sam and David Michael worked on the ghost.

Kristy and I made a monster. We found a scary rubber mask. We hung it on the wall. We put a flashlight behind it. When we turned on the light, the monster face began to glow.

"Let's make a spookhouse tape," suggested Charlie.

David Michael found the tape recorder.

He taped Andrew screaming. He taped Kristy rattling some chains. He taped Charlie clomping up the stairs. He taped Sam wailing like a ghost. He taped me cackling like a witch. At the end of the tape, we all yelled, "BOO!"

"This is going to be the spookiest spookhouse," said Andrew.

David Michael flicked on the tape we had made. *Aughhhhh! Rattle-rattle. Clomp, clomp, clomp. Ooooo-ooooh. Heh-heh-heh. BOO!*

"Yipes!" cried Andrew.

"Let's play it for Emily," suggested David Michael. So we did. (Emily laughed.)

"Dinnertime!" called Daddy.

I did not eat much dinner. Just a hamburger bun.

"Oh," said Nannie, "you have to eat better than that if you want Halloween candy tomorrow."

"But I'm not hungry," I replied. Besides, I was getting nervous about the next night. I had tried not to think about Druscilla's party. But in twenty-four hours I would have to go to it. I would be in the witches' house.

"Can I be excused?" I asked.

Daddy said yes. I stood up and whispered something to Andrew.

"Okay!" cried Andrew.

My brother and I ran to our playroom. In the box of dress-up clothes we found two more scary masks. We put them on. Then we went back to the kitchen. The rest of our family was still sitting at the table.

"What's this?" Elizabeth wanted to know, when she saw Andrew and me.

Andrew and I jumped forward. *"I was working in my lab late one night,"* I sang. (Andrew sang, *"I was working on my slab . . ."*)

We performed the song. When we finished, our family clapped for us. Then I went to my room. Believe me. I remembered the No Spying rule. But I just *had* to spy on the witches' house. It was for my own safety.

I turned out the light in the bedroom. I looked in a window at Morbidda's house.

There was Druscilla! She was playing with Midnight. Wait! She was dangling a toy in front of him. The toy swung back and forth. The little witch was hypnotizing the black cat!

17

The Face at the Window

On Halloween, I tried very hard not to think about Druscilla's party. Instead, I put on my costume again. I invited Hannie over. I showed her everything in our spookhouse. Sam showed her how he could make the ghost float up and down the staircase. Then Elizabeth let us put the Halloween candy in a basket for the trick-or-treaters. (Hannie and I hardly sampled any of it. Just a few tastes to be sure the candy was okay.)

Late in the afternoon, Kristy called, "Who's ready to go trick-or-treating?"

"Me!" shouted David Michael and Andrew and Emily and I.

We made sure our costumes looked just right. Then I found my "trick-or-treat-for-the-hospital box." Soon the doorbell rang.

"That's Mary Anne!" called Kristy. (Kristy has a good friend named Mary Anne. She is a baby-sitter, too. She was going to help with trick-or-treating. That was because *nine* kids were going out. Even Kristy could not watch nine kids by herself.)

We stopped by Hannie's house. We picked up Hannie, Linny, and Sari. (Mrs. Papadakis handed out boxes of Cracker Jacks.) Then we stopped by Melody's house. We picked up Melody and her older brother, Bill. (Mr. Korman handed out Butterfinger bars.)

"Okay. Let's get going!" said Kristy.

My friends and I walked down our street.

The sky had grown black. Dry leaves whisked around our feet. I looked past the bare branches of a tree. "Maybe the moon will be full tonight," I said.

Nobody answered. We tiptoed to the doorway of a house.

"I think this is a ghost house," I said.

David Michael rang the bell anyway.

The door flew open. An old man gave each of us a package of gum.

Hannie and Linny and I stuck out our boxes. "Trick-or-treat for the hospital!" we cried.

"How nice," said the man. He smiled. He dropped a quarter into each box.

"Thanks!" we said.

"Yum! Gum!" exclaimed Emily. She peered into her bag. She looked surprised.

At the next house, Emily ran ahead of us. She reached the door before anyone else. She tried to ring the bell. When someone answered the door, she stuck her bag right out. "Candy!" she said happily.

Emily became a champion trick-ortreater. She did not seem to notice how scary everything was. She did not care when I said that a house was haunted. She did not care when I thought I saw a skeleton. Or when we walked by a tree that looked like a hiding place for goblins. . . . Or when we climbed the steps to someone's front porch and I saw *a face at the window.*

"Yipes!" I shrieked. "A face!"

The face belonged to the man who lived in the house. He opened his door. He gave us each a package of licorice sticks.

"Trick-or-treat for the hospital?" said Linny.

"You are the fourth one to ask," replied the man. He closed his door.

"Meanie-mo," I whispered.

Trick-or-treating was gigundoly fun. Except for the mean man. And except for when Emily's bag broke and all her candy fell out. And except for every time I thought about the witches' party. When I got home, I raced upstairs with my bag and my box. I counted my candy. Then I counted the money for the hospital. "Not bad!" I told myself.

"Karen!" called Daddy then. "Time to go to the party!"

Oh, boo.

18

The Pumpkin People

*D*um, *da-dum, dum.*

Witching time.

I only bothered to say, "Do I *have* to go, Daddy?" once. That was because Daddy's answer was, "Yes." I knew he meant it.

Kristy's friend had gone home. So Kristy walked me next door to Druscilla's house. I walked as slowly as I could.

When we were standing on the front steps, I announced, "I am not going in there without Hannie and Melody."

Kristy sighed. She rang the doorbell.

Eeek! *Morbidda Destiny* answered it.

But guess what. She was wearing a Halloween costume. She was dressed like a fat pumpkin. She did not look scary at all.

"Happy Halloween, Karen," said Mrs. Porter. "Come inside."

I peeked around Mrs. Porter. In the hallway behind her were a bunch of kids. Hannie and Melody were with them. They did not look sick. Or bewitched. They looked like they might be having fun.

"Do you want me to come in with you?" Kristy whispered.

"No, thanks. That's okay. I think I can go by myself."

"Okay. Have a good time." Kristy walked back to the big house.

I stepped inside. I walked by Mrs. Porter. Druscilla ran to meet me.

"Hi, Karen!" she called. Druscilla was wearing a pumpkin costume, too.

Well, for heaven's sake. There was *nothing* scary here.

The party was held in the living room.

Orange streamers hung from the ceiling. Smiling pumpkins sat on the floor. On a table were bowls of pretzels and potato chips and candy corn. And a pitcher of juice. Some kids were bobbing for apples.

"Do you want to bob for apples?" asked Druscilla. "Or paint pumpkin faces? Everyone gets their own pumpkin. You can paint over there. See those paints? You can even wear a smock, if you want."

"We each get our own pumpkin?" I repeated.

"Yup," said Druscilla.

Amazing.

Hannie and Melody and I chose pumpkins. We painted faces on them.

"This is fun!" said Melody.

Yeah. Too much fun. Where were the mushroom cakes? Where were the herb cookies? Where was the witch's brew?

"Time for cupcakes!" Mrs. Porter said then.

"Aha!" I hissed. "They're *enchanted* cupcakes. I just know it."

Hannie and Melody and I ran to Mrs. Porter. We examined the tray of cupcakes she was carrying. The cupcakes were decorated to look like jack-o'-lanterns. "Just as I thought," I murmured.

Melody and Hannie did not pay any attention to me. They each took a cupcake.

"You'll be sorry," I warned them.

But my friends just said, "Oh, yum!"

So I ate a cupcake, too. If it put a spell on me, I did not know about it. Nothing happened. I felt fine. (I ate a second cupcake.)

After cupcakes, we played musical chairs. Melody won. Mrs. Porter gave her a pencil with a silly ghost where the eraser should have been.

Then we ran around and played hide-and-seek.

Before I knew it, Mrs. Porter was saying, "Children, it's nine o'clock."

Halloween Night

Nine o'clock! That meant the party was over. How could it be over so fast? I felt as if I had just arrived.

The doorbell rang then. Mr. Korman had come to pick up Melody. Other parents began to drop by. Soon Daddy arrived.

When I saw him at the door, I ran to him. "Daddy!" I cried. "We had so much fun! We painted pumpkins! Look!" I dragged Daddy into the living room. I showed him the row of painted faces. "There's the one

I did," I said proudly. "And I get to bring it home."

I picked up my pumpkin. Mrs. Porter handed me a small goody bag.

"Thank you," I said. "And thank you for the nice party." I turned to Druscilla. "Do you want to come over and play tomorrow?" I asked her.

Druscilla grinned. "Sure!"

"Goody. Come in the morning, okay?"

"Okay. 'Bye, Karen."

" 'Bye!"

Daddy and I walked through the cold, dark night. "Halloween is over," I said. "Over for a whole year. That spooky feeling is gone."

"Are you glad?" asked Daddy.

"No! I like being scared. Sort of."

When we reached the big house, I went to my room. I flopped on my bed. I began to take off my Pippi costume. I felt sort of sad. But I was not sure why.

Then I realized something. I felt the way I sometimes feel on Christmas night. The holiday was over. The excitement was over.

"No more Halloween until next year," I said to myself. I wished it were a week earlier. Then I could look forward to Halloween all over again.

I picked up Moosie. "What do you think I should be for Halloween next year?" I asked him. I held him to my ear. "What?" I said. "A witch again? Well, maybe I will do that. I miss my witch costume."

I pulled out my bag of Halloween candy. I had hidden it under my bed. I did not want anyone to snitch from it. "Would you like a candy bar?" I asked Moosie. "No? Okay, then I will have one." I began to peel the paper off of a Mars bar. Then I thought about what I had eaten that day. Aside from breakfast, lunch, and a small supper, I had eaten a handful of candy corn, a Snickers bar, a root beer barrel, two cupcakes, a lot of potato chips, and a few pretzels. Also, I had chewed a pack of gum.

I put the Mars bar back in my bag. I could eat it the next day.

I was about to hide the bag again when I decided that I should organize my loot. First I made piles for the different kinds of candy. But there were too many piles. Then I put all the big candy in one pile, and the little candy in another pile. I did not like the way that looked.

So I threw the candy back in the bag and hid it in my closet. Then I changed into my nightgown. I climbed into bed.

"Come say good night to me!" I yelled.

When Daddy and Elizabeth and Kristy and Nannie had kissed me good night, I sat up. I looked out my window.

I looked at the witch house next door. I thought of Druscilla and her grandmother dressed like pumpkin people. I could not imagine pumpkin people flying on broomsticks or casting spells. I decided that Mrs. Porter and Druscilla were probably just regular people.

You know what? I missed having witches next door to me.

20

November

When I woke up the next morning, I remembered to say, "Rabbit, rabbit," first thing. You are supposed to say that at the beginning of each month. Sam said so. (But I do not know why.)

"It's November," I told myself. First I felt sad again. Halloween was over. But then I cheered up. If Halloween was over, then other holidays were just beginning. First would come Thanksgiving. Then Christmas. Then New Year's Eve. And then Valentine's Day!

"Oh, boy!" I cried. "Turkey! Presents! Staying up till midnight! Cards and candy!" I leaped out of bed.

I ran downstairs to have breakfast. While I poured my cereal, I said, "Do you guys know what I am going to be for Halloween next year?"

"I can't believe you are thinking about that," said Sam. (Often, Sam is grumpy in the morning. I never sit near him.)

"I am going to be a witch again."

"Goody," said Sam.

I stuck my tongue out at him.

When breakfast was over I went back to my room. I needed to find a better hiding place for my candy. I had decided the closet was not good enough.

I was stuffing the bag behind my bookcase when Elizabeth called, "Karen! Dru is here! She's on her way up!"

Yipes! I had forgotten I'd invited Druscilla over to play. I tried to get my candy hidden before Druscilla reached my room. I did not make it.

"Ooh," said Druscilla. "Look at all that candy. Wow. I did not go trick-or-treating. I was too busy getting ready for the party."

I felt bad. I handed Druscilla a chocolate bar. I took one for myself.

Druscilla sat on my bed. Her pumpkin costume was gone, of course. She was wearing her black clothes again. She looked a little more . . . witchy.

I shivered.

"Did you like the party?" asked Druscilla.

I nodded. "Yup. It was fun. Look. There's my pumpkin. I am going to keep it on my desk until it gets smelly."

Druscilla smiled.

"Um . . . I liked the cupcakes, too," I added.

"Thanks."

"Maybe you can go trick-or-treating next year."

"Maybe."

I thought for awhile. I wanted to ask Druscilla a certain question very badly. I really needed to know the answer.

I took a deep breath. "Are you *really* a witch, Druscilla?" I hoped she was not embarrassed.

Druscilla lowered her eyes. "No," she admitted. "I made that up."

"But why?"

"Because I thought you *wanted* me to be a witch."

"Oh. . . ."

"But," Druscilla went on, "you can never tell about my grandmother."

My mouth dropped open. What did that mean? Was Morbidda Destiny a witch after all? If she was, then Druscilla must be a witch, too.

Yipes! I was sitting in my bedroom with a little witch!

Wasn't I?

I wondered if I would ever know the truth.

About the Author

ANN M. MARTIN lives in New York City and loves animals, especially cats. She has two cats of her own, Mouse and Rosie.

Other books by Ann M. Martin that you might enjoy are *Stage Fright*; *Me and Katie (the Pest)*; and the books in *The Baby-sitters Club* series.

Ann likes ice cream and *I Love Lucy*. And she has her own little sister, whose name is Jane.

Little Sister

Don't miss #23

KAREN'S DOLL

The morning went really fast. In no time, I heard Ms. Colman announcing Show and Share. It was time to introduce Hyacynthia.

When I picked her up from her basket, everyone was gigundo impressed. I heard some of the girls say, "Wow!" You should have seen Pamela Harding's face. And Ricky whistled at her. (The boys may have thought he was joking. But I knew he liked her.)

"My grandma and grandpa brought Hyacynthia all the way from England," I said.

"She was just a baby doll without a name when they brought her. Then my good friend Nancy, who is absent today, named her."

I wrote my doll's name in big letters on the blackboard, so no one would forget.

Kristy is Karen's older stepsister, and she and her friends are...

by Ann M. Martin, author of *Baby-sitters Little Sister*™

Available wherever you buy books, or use this order form.

What Katy Did
Reading Questions

- What sorts of things do Katy and her siblings do for fun? How do they differ from the things that modern children do for entertainment?

- In what ways is Katy changed by her accident? What does she learn from the "School of Pain"?

- How does Katy make herself important to the family after she is confined to her bed?

- Near the beginning of the book, Katy talks about doing "something grand" with her life. What do you think will happen to Katy now that the story is over?